SCHOOL SPOOKS DAY

'*Go!*' screamed the PE teacher, Ms Legg,
over the sound of the starter's pistol.

Lenny launched himself forwards. The race
would all be over in a matter of seconds, and
this was the best opportunity to secure a lead.

Lenny focused on the red tape of the finish
line ahead, fluttering in the wind. He could
hear feet thumping into the ground behind him.

Suddenly, a ghost shot up from the grass in
front of him, playing some sort of musical
instrument made of rib bones.

Lenny jumped and landed awkwardly, twisting
his ankle and crashing to the ground.

Luke Thomas leapt over him and burst across
the finish line, and Lenny watched as the musical
spirit sent the crowd running and screaming.

The attack had begun.

D1113604

St Sebastian's School in Grimesford is the pits. No, really – it is.

Every year, the high school sinks a bit further into the boggy plague pit beneath it and, every year, the ghosts of the plague victims buried underneath it become a bit more cranky.

Egged on by their spooky ringleader, Edith Codd, they decide to get their own back – and they're willing to play dirty. *Really* dirty.

They kick up a stink by causing as much mischief as in inhumanly possible so as to get St Sebastian's closed down once and for all.

But what they haven't reckoned on is year-seven new boy, James Simpson and his friends Alexander and Lenny.

The question is, are the gang up to the challenge of laying St Sebastian's paranormal problem to rest, or will their school remain forever frightful?

There's only one way to find out . . .

www.too-ghoul.com

SCHOOL
SPOOKS
DAY

B. STRANGE

EGMONT

Special thanks to:

Tommy Donbavand, St John's Walworth Church of England Primary School and Belmont Primary School

EGMONT

We bring stories to life

Published in Great Britain 2007
by Egmont UK Limited
239 Kensington High Street, London W8 6SA

Text & illustrations © 2007 Egmont UK Ltd
Text by Tommy Donbavand
Illustrations by Pulsar Studio (Beehive Illustration)

ISBN 978 1 4052 3237 1

1 3 5 7 9 10 8 6 4 2

A CIP catalogue record for this title is available
from the British Library

Typeset by Avon DataSet Ltd, Bidford on Avon, Warwickshire
Printed and bound in Great Britain by the CPI Group

'More books – I love it!'
Ashley, age 11

'It's disgusting. . .'
Joe, age 10

'. . . it's all good!'
Alexander, age 9

'. . . loads of excitement and really gross!'
Jay, age 9

'I like the way there's the brainy boy,
the brawny boy and the cool boy that form a
team of friends'
Charlie, age 10

'That ghost Edith is wicked'
Matthew, age 11

'This is really good and funny!'
Sam, age 9

...Ghoul!

Loud-mouthed ringleader of the plague-pit ghosts

Edith Codd

Young ghost and a secret wannabe St Sebastian's pupil

William Scroggins

Bone idle ex-leech merchant with a taste for all things gross

Ambrose Harbottle

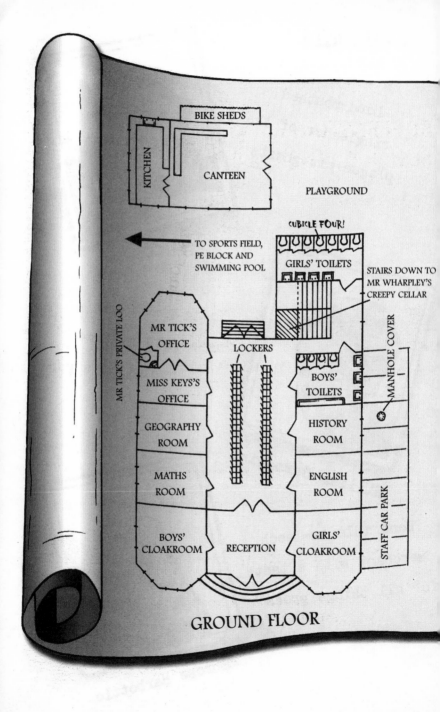

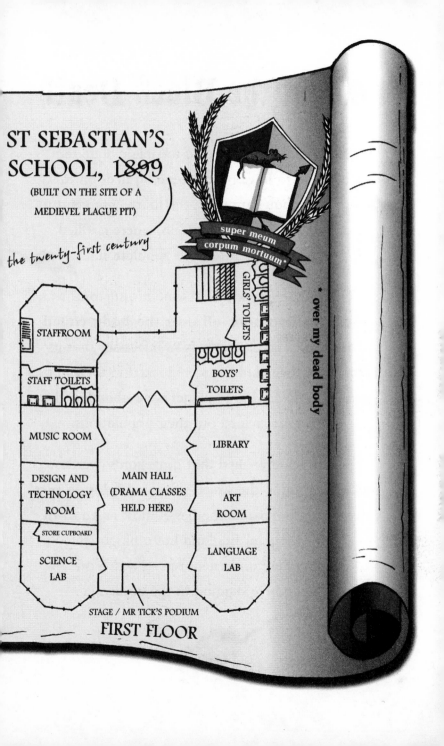

About the Black Death

The Black Death was a terrible plague that is believed to have been spread by fleas on rats. It swept through Europe in the fourteenth century, arriving in England in 1348, where it killed over one third of the population.

One of the Black Death's main symptoms was **foul-smelling boils all over the body called 'buboes'**. The plague was so infectious that its victims and their families were locked in their houses until they died. Many villages were abandoned as the disease wiped out their populations.

So many people died that graveyards overflowed and bodies lay in the street, so special **'plague pits'** were dug to bury the bodies. Almost every town and village in England has a plague pit somewhere underneath it, so watch out when you're digging in the garden . . .

Dear Reader

As you may have already guessed, B. Strange is not a real name.

The author of this series is an ex-teacher who is currently employed by a little-known body called the Organisation For Spook Termination (Excluding Demons), or O.F.S.T.(E.D.). 'B. Strange' is the pen name chosen to protect his identity.

Together, we felt it was our duty to publish these books, in an attempt to save innocent lives. The stories are based on the author's experiences as an O.F.S.T.(E.D.) inspector in various schools over the past two decades.

Please read them carefully – you may regret it if you don't . . .

Yours sincerely
The Publisher.

PS – Should you wish to file a report on any suspicious supernatural occurrences at your school, visit **www.too-ghoul.com** and fill out the relevant form. We'll pass it on to O.F.S.T.(E.D.) for you.

PPS – All characters' names have been changed to protect the identity of the individuals. Any similarity to actual persons, living or undead, is purely coincidental.

CONTENTS

ELVIS PRESLEY

The American singer Elvis Presley is mentioned quite a few times in *School Spooks Day* (Mr Wharpley, the school caretaker, has a huge collection of his records).

Here are some interesting facts about Elvis:

- He was born in 1935 and died in 1977
- He is often called 'The King of Rock 'n' Roll'!
- He wiggled his hips when he was singing – older people thought this was disgusting!
- He once shot a TV set with a gun because he didn't like the show that was on!
- He was one of the most famous performers of the twentieth century, and is reported to have sold over one billion singles and albums, which would make him the biggest-selling solo artist of all time!

CHAPTER 1
SWAMPED

'U-huh-huh,' crooned Mr Wharpley, caretaker of St Sebastian's School, and owner of the world's greasiest hairstyle. He'd tried to shape it into an Elvis-style quiff, but the gunk from the school kitchen's deep-fat fryer just didn't work as well as real hair gel, and his fringe flopped about like a dead rat.

Picturing himself as his hero, Mr Wharpley spun the mop around to use it as a microphone, but mistimed the move and slapped himself in the face with the sopping wet sponge.

Spluttering, he quickly looked around the changing rooms of the school's indoor swimming pool to make sure no one had seen the incident. Certain that he was alone, he whipped a master key from his shirt pocket, used it to open a nearby locker, and grabbed the clean trunks of a year-eight boy to dry his face.

Slamming the locker closed, Mr Wharpley spun the volume control of his ancient CD player as 'Hound Dog', his favourite Elvis tune of all time, began to ring out. He sang along, gyrating his hips in a way he believed made him look like The King of Rock 'n' Roll but, in reality, gave the impression that his underwear was full of itching powder.

Suddenly, there was a loud clanking sound, followed by a grating of metal on metal that set the caretaker's teeth on edge.

'What *now*?' he moaned, using the handle of his mop to switch off Elvis. He went in the direction of the pool, taking care to avoid the footbath as he left the changing room. No point cleaning his boots twice in one month.

Mr Wharpley stood at the side of the swimming pool and gazed into the water. Something wasn't right, but he couldn't quite put his finger on it. The water was clean, the broken tiles had been repaired, and the swimming lanes had been repainted on the bottom with paint he was almost certain wouldn't be poisonous if swallowed. The water looked perfectly clear and still.

Perfectly clear and still. That was it. The flippin' pool filter had packed up! It was supposed to constantly drain whatever mess the little brats left in there and churn out clean water to replace it, but it had stopped.

The caretaker shuffled around the edge of the pool to the machine room on the far side. 'Make sure everything's ready for school sports day,

Mr Wharpley!' he whined, imitating the headmaster, Mr Tick. 'Everything has to be perfect for when the parents arrive!'

'The only way this school will be perfect is if we get rid of the little monsters that make my life a misery every day!' Mr Wharpley allowed himself a little smile at the wondrous thought of a school with no pupils as he searched his pockets for the key to the machine room.

Unlocking the door and tugging it open, he stared in horror at the mess in front of him. A metal lifesaving pole had fallen from its place on the wall and jammed in the cogs of the ancient pool filter. Despite clear instructions from health and safety that the lifesaving equipment needed to be available at all times, Mr Wharpley kept it all locked safely away in the machine room. He was now beginning to regret the decision.

Grabbing the handle, he tried to pull the pole free of the machine into which it was jammed.

It wouldn't move. Perhaps if he pressed his foot against the side of the filter to get a better grip? The elderly man raised a dirty boot and pushed hard while yanking at the pole. Yes! . . . The cogs were starting to turn.

In one swift movement, Mr Wharpley's foot slipped off the side of the filter and swung upwards, whereupon the turn-ups of his right trouser leg became caught in the machinery along with the pole.

'Oh, great!' groaned the caretaker, hopping on his free foot to try and stay upright. He let go of the pole with one hand and stretched out to try and free his leg. These trousers were only twelve years old, he had to be careful not to rip them.

Suddenly, the cogs jerked forwards a little more, snagging the left sleeve of his shirt in their teeth, along with the pole and his trousers.

'Oh, for flip's sake!' yelled Mr Wharpley. He would never live it down if anyone came in and

found him like this. He had to escape from the
clutches of the pool filter.

With his free hand, the caretaker gripped the
largest of the cogs and tried to turn it. The metal
teeth bit into his fingers as he slowly . . . ever so
slowly . . . began to spin the cog around . . .

That was when the foot he was balancing on slipped from underneath him and Mr Wharpley spun upside down. His favourite tie – the one with the orange and brown spanner print on it – caught in between the cogs and pulled tight as the caretaker fell to the floor.

'Kkkxxggghhh!' gurgled the angry caretaker as the tie threatened to cut off his air supply. He . . . had . . . to . . . free . . . himself . . .

There was only one option left open: switch the filter to reverse. That way, he would have a second or so to pull his shirt, trousers and tie clear of the machinery as the cogs began to turn the opposite way. The problem was, he couldn't reach the lever with his one free arm. That just left his mouth.

Gripping the handle between his teeth – and cursing himself for buying such foul-tasting polish – Mr Wharpley pulled down hard on the lever. It had been years since the filter had been run in reverse, and the handle was rusted in place. The caretaker gripped tight and pulled even harder.

The lever didn't move for a few seconds. Then, suddenly, it slammed into the reverse position, sending the cogs of the filter spinning in the opposite direction.

Mr Wharpley's trousers, shirt and tie came free and he fell backwards, grabbing for the handle of the pool pole. The pole came free of the cogs and fell away from the machine as the caretaker was catapulted backwards through the machine-room door and into the swimming pool with a splash.

Spluttering, Mr Wharpley made it back to the surface of the water just in time to see generations of slime, hair and sticking plasters come belching out of the grilles around the edges of the pool. Within seconds, the caretaker was swimming in what appeared to be a swamp filled with dead skin, scabs, rotting earplugs and old toenails.

Mr Wharpley spat out a mouldy verruca sock and shuddered as he paddled wildly to stay above the now crusty surface of the pool.

Elvis had never gone through anything like this.

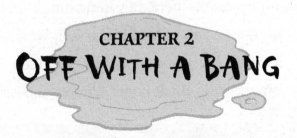

CHAPTER 2
OFF WITH A BANG

'Is this on?' asked Mr Tick the following
morning, patting the microphone that had been
set up in front of his podium and sending out
squeals of feedback. The St Sebastian's staff,
pupils and their parents assembled in front of
him on the school sports field clamped their
hands over their ears.

Year-seven pupil, James Simpson, stood at the
back of the crowd with his friend Lenny
Maxwell. 'Well, they've picked a great day for it,'
he joked, glancing up at the grey, drizzling sky.

'Couldn't be nicer,' agreed Lenny, pulling his collar up against the sharp wind that was whistling across the field. His huge hands stuck out from the sleeves of his blazer; they were blue with the cold. Most of the people surrounding him were wearing thick coats, scarves and gloves.

'I'm not happy about this!' complained a voice, causing James and Lenny to turn around. They struggled to contain their laughter as their friend, Alexander Tick, approached, dressed in the skimpiest T-shirt and shorts the boys had ever seen. 'Not happy about this at all!'

'Well, what do you know,' said James, gesturing to Alexander's thin, goose-pimple-covered body. 'They've hired a professional weightlifter to get things going!'

'Very *funny*!' moaned Alexander, jumping on the spot to try and stop himself from trembling with the cold. 'I'll have you know that I'm built for intelligence, not sport!'

'You can say that again,' smiled Lenny. 'If I had legs like yours, I'd walk on my arms.'

'Shhh!' demanded Alexander. 'My dad's starting his speech and he'll know if I haven't listened.'

'How?' asked James.

Alexander pulled a face. 'He's going to test me on what he said,' he groaned.

James bit his lip to disguise yet another laugh, and concentrated on listening to the headmaster.

'I would like to welcome you one and all to St Sebastian's sports day!' announced Mr Tick, via the crackling microphone.

The teachers to the side of him attempted to begin a round of applause, but no one else joined in.

'I am delighted to have made available the swimming pool for today's events,' continued the headmaster. Unfortunately, because of the microphone cutting in and out, his words came out of the speakers sounding like 'I am . . . made av . . . poo . . .'

James turned to Alexander. 'Did your dad just tell everyone he's made of poo?' he asked.

Alexander shrugged. 'He said it was going to be a different speech this year, but I didn't think he meant *that* different.'

James removed his school blazer and handed it to a grateful Alexander. 'You're starting to turn blue,' he explained.

'Mr Wharpley is working to ensure there will be no upheaval if we have to move indoors due to the weather,' continued Mr Tick from his podium. Again the microphone crackled, so what everyone actually heard was: 'Mr Wharpley is . . . eaval . . .'

'Mr Wharpley is evil?' repeated James. 'The truth is out at last!'

'He's right, too,' added Lenny. 'I saw him on the way home last night and he looked terrible. He was soaking wet and his hair was covered with old plasters and bits of tissue.'

Alexander shook his head. 'I think it's the microphone,' he said. 'It's cutting in and out, so we can only hear part of what my dad's saying.'

James sighed. 'Thanks for that, Sherlock,' he teased.

'Quiet!' hissed Lenny. 'I think he's just said that Mr Watts will be performing cartwheels while dressed as a chicken.'

James shook his head. 'No, he definitely said he's heading out west for a kicking!' Both he and Lenny dissolved into fits of giggles.

Alexander scowled. 'Thanks, guys,' he said. 'I'll be sure to mention your comments to him.'

'Oh, stop your moaning!' James said, nudging him in the ribs. 'It's nearly time for your event. I reckon there's a good chance you'll break the record in this year's one-hundred-metre algebra.'

Lenny nodded. 'He's up for the long-division jump, too!' Once again, both James and Lenny collapsed with laughter.

'You two can scoff,' sneered Alexander. 'But we Ticks will have the last laugh: I know how long my dad's speeches can go on for.'

Twenty-five minutes later, James, Lenny and Alexander were lying on the damp grass, willing Mr Tick to stop talking.

'Can't we just go up and unplug his microphone?' groaned Lenny.

'That stopped working ten minutes ago,' said James. 'Didn't put him off at all.'

A smattering of polite applause caught the boys' attention. Alexander stood up and peered over the top of the now restless crowd. 'He's finished.'

'At last,' said James, getting to his feet and massaging his aching legs. 'What's on now?'

Lenny pulled a poorly photocopied sports-day programme out of his pocket and looked down the list. 'Display by the St Sebastian's cheerleaders,' he said.

It was Alexander's turn to nudge James now. 'Stacey Carmichael's performing,' he said. 'Do you want to go up to the front so you can get a better view?'

James blushed deeply. 'Don't know what you're talking about,' he muttered, staring down at his feet as he dug his toes into the muddy grass.

'Oh, come on, Romeo,' laughed Lenny, wrapping an arm around his friend.

James pushed him away. 'Get off!' he growled. 'We're staying back here!'

'It doesn't matter,' announced Alexander, beaming. 'They're coming this way!'

James's cheeks flushed a deeper red as a dozen girls ran in their direction, casting off their coats to reveal blue and yellow cheerleading outfits. Stacey Carmichael groaned when she saw the

boys and threw them a look that instantly made them feel like blundering five-year-olds.

'Hello, James!' she shouted teasingly, her short skirt billowing in the wind.

'Mmph,' mumbled James in return.

'OK, girls!' shouted Ms Legg, the PE teacher, from the podium. 'After four . . .' She pressed the 'play' button on a CD player that was connected to the sound system.

Leandra Maxwell, Lenny's older sister, took her place at the front of the squad and counted aloud. 'One, two, three, four!'

The cheerleaders gripped their pompoms and began to dance as noisy pop music blared out of the speakers and echoed across the sports field.

'Give me an S!' shouted Leandra.

'S!' replied the dancers.

'Give me an A!' Leandra yelled.

'A!' came the response.

'Give me an I!' called Leandra.

'I!' sang the girls.

Alexander leant in to Lenny. 'This could take a while,' he whispered.

Lenny grinned and turned to James to share the joke, but his friend was staring, transfixed by the sight of Stacey Carmichael dancing to the music.

'Houston, we have a problem!' said Lenny, tapping Alexander on the shoulder and gesturing to James.

The headmaster's son giggled. 'I think he's blown a fuse!' he said.

Lenny nodded his agreement. 'I don't think anything can break his concentration!'

Suddenly, there was a scream as Leandra performed one of the dance moves wrong and, swinging out her pompom-filled hand, she punched Stacey in the side of the head, sending the blonde girl crashing to the ground.

James stared, open-mouthed.

'Apart from *that*, of course,' said Lenny.

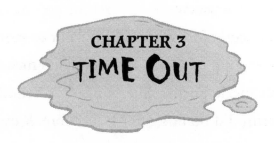

CHAPTER 3
TIME OUT

Along with concerned parents and pupils, James dashed over to where Stacey Carmichael lay sobbing on the wet grass.

'Are you OK?' he asked.

Stacey looked up at him through tear-filled eyes. 'J-James?' she stammered, reaching out for his hand. 'Is that you?'

James allowed her to squeeze his fingers once before he pulled his hand away, suddenly aware that they were surrounded by people. Leandra arrived carrying Stacey's coat.

'I'm so sorry!' she said, wrapping the jacket around her friend's shoulders.

Stacey glanced up to check that no one else was looking before opening her coat to reveal the latest copy of *Cool Goss* magazine tucked into her inside pocket. She winked at Leandra.

'I'm sure I'll be fine after a little break away from this cold, wet sports field, Leandra!' she whimpered.

Leandra grinned, shaking her head. 'I *knew* I wasn't in the wrong place!' she whispered. 'It was *you*!'

'Move back, everyone!' commanded a voice. Ms Legg pushed her way through the crowd. 'Are your parents here, Stacey?'

'No, miss,' sobbed Stacey, turning on the tears again. 'They wanted to come *so* much, but they're both at work today.'

Ms Legg breathed a sigh of relief. 'Well, that's something,' she said. 'Can you walk?'

'I–I think so, miss,' Stacey blubbed, as the PE teacher helped her to stand.

'Let's get you back to the changing room so you can put your feet up for a while,' said Ms Legg.

James watched, as the teacher helped Stacey off the field. He sighed, wishing briefly he was the one with his arm around the injured cheerleader.

His dreams were shattered as another deafening blast of feedback screeched out from Mr Tick's microphone.

'Well, let's get back to the sports day! We're ready to start the track events, if no one grumbles about the weather!' the headmaster said, noticing the concerned faces of the parents all around him.

Unfortunately, his crackling microphone kicked in and all that anyone heard was: 'Let's get . . . ready to . . . rumble . . .'

Stacey slumped back against one of the benches in the changing room and clutched at the side of her head dramatically.

'Are you *sure* you don't want me to call an ambulance?' asked Ms Legg, concerned.

'No!' blurted Stacey, making a mental note to tone down the acting. She'd have some explaining to do if she ended up in hospital. 'I just need to sit here in the warm until my head clears a bit, miss.'

Ms Legg frowned. 'I'm not sure I should be leaving you alone.'

'I'll be fine, Ms Legg,' said Stacey, flashing the smile that ensured she always got her way with the boys at St Sebastian's. She hoped it would work with the teachers, too.

'How many fingers am I holding up?' the teacher asked.

Stacey sighed. Ms Legg was obviously harder to fool than an eleven-year-old boy. This was going to take a little more work.

'Er, six, miss?' whined Stacey, doubling the number of fingers that had been thrust in front of her face.

'That does it,' said Ms Legg. 'I'm going to ask Miss Keys to call your parents so that one of them can come and collect you. You should be at home, in bed.'

Stacey did a mental cartwheel of joy. Result! Not only was she getting out of sports day, she could spend the rest of the afternoon in bed, listening to music and reading magazines. Better keep up the pretence though.

'Does that mean I'll have to miss the rest of sports day?' she asked in a quiet voice.

'I'm afraid so, Stacey,' answered Ms Legg. 'You may be suffering from a slight concussion and it's best that you take the rest of the day off and rest.'

Stacey did her best to look upset. 'And I was *so* looking forward to running the fifteen-hundred-metres, miss!' she moaned, shivering as she pictured herself racing around a muddy track in the cold and wet.

'Well, you stay here, and I'll be back with Miss Keys,' said the teacher, heading out of the changing room.

Stacey waited for a few seconds, just to make sure that Ms Legg wasn't coming straight back in, then she pulled out her copy of *Cool Goss* and settled back to read.

'Oh, yes, Stacey,' she said aloud, 'you've still got it!'

She flicked past the pages of make-up tips – as if she would ever need any help in *that* department – to her favourite section of the magazine: the agony column.

Absorbed in the problems of the magazine's readers, time passed Stacey by until –

What was that?

Stacey sat bolt upright, as a hissing noise echoed out across the changing room. Maybe she wasn't alone after all.

'Hello?' she called out. 'Is there anybody there?'

The hissing noise had gone. The changing room was silent again for a moment before Stacey heard another noise: bubbling.

'Who's there?' she shouted. 'Gordon Carver, if that's you . . . I'll tell Ms Legg you're in the girls' changing room again!'

The bubbling noise continued. It was coming from the toilet.

'I mean it!' Stacey yelled. 'This isn't funny! Stop it *right now*!'

The bubbling became louder.

Putting down her magazine, Stacey cautiously tiptoed over to the cubicle and, after taking a deep breath, pushed open the door. The water inside the toilet bowl was churning about furiously.

Stacey held her breath. What was going on? Perhaps the bad weather was affecting the pipes, or maybe Mr Wharpley was doing some work down in the cellar?

'If I flush the toilet, it might stop,' she told herself.

Trembling slightly, Stacey reached out for the handle. She gripped it and was about to push down when something – no, some*one* – shot up

out of the water and vanished into thin air.

Stacey fell back with a scream, landing hard on the tiled floor of the changing room. What on earth was *that*? She reached up and gently touched the side of her head where Leandra had hit her.

'Maybe I *am* concussed after all!' she said, puzzled.

CHAPTER 4
MAKING AN APPEARANCE

'She saw me!' William Scroggins held his breath, which was a particularly impressive thing to do as he was dead and hadn't actually taken one for over six hundred years.

He had floated up through the pipes from the sewer below, fully expecting the changing room to be empty, but there had been a girl watching him as he appeared from the toilet.

He had instantly turned himself invisible, of course. The ghosts of the plague pit beneath the school had strict rules about not allowing pupils or staff to see them. Or, rather, Edith Codd, their overbearing leader had that strict rule, and everyone else went along with it for fear of being bullied.

William floated a metre above the toilet bowl, invisible to the girl who had collapsed backwards when he had first appeared, and studied her.

It was Stacey! He had seen this girl before, and she was beautiful. The prettiest girl he had ever seen, in fact. Her eyes were as blue as periwinkles and her hair as golden as a florin – no, a whole bagful of florins! William watched as she clambered to her feet and sat on one of the benches.

'Pull yourself together, Stacey!' she said aloud.

William sighed at the melodic sound of her voice. He allowed himself to float down to the floor. As a ghost, William didn't actually need to walk on the ground, but he felt sick if he hovered in the air for too long and using his legs to get about was a welcome reminder of his short time alive.

He turned his attentions back to Stacey. She was was busy getting changed.

Getting changed! If William's transparent cheeks could have altered colour, they would have blushed a deep red. He had to get out of here. It wasn't right that he was watching her like this.

In one swift movement, William dived back into the toilet bowl and slid down through the pipes underneath.

'Did you do it?' demanded Edith, as soon as William appeared in the sewer that the plague-pit ghosts called home.

'Do what?' asked William, trying to get the image of Stacey out of his mind.

Edith growled.

'Did you find out if their ridiculous sports day has started?' she thundered. 'You *know* the sewer pipes don't stretch out as far as the playing fields and I can't listen in to what they're doing!'

William's expression froze. The sports day. He knew there'd been a reason for him to visit the school, but he'd forgotten all about it when he'd seen Stacey.

'They, er – They haven't quite started yet,' he said, trying not to trip over his words. 'The weather's not too good.'

'The weather!' spat Edith. 'Always moaning about the weather! They'd complain a whole lot more if they were dead and couldn't even *feel* the weather, like me! What I wouldn't give to run naked in the rain one more time!'

William screwed his eyes closed and tried to push the revolting image of Edith running around without her clothes from his mind.

'So, you want me to go up again?' he asked.

Edith nodded. 'And don't come back until that stupid sports day is well and truly under way!' she snapped.

As William disappeared back up the pipe, Edith shouted after him: 'Today is the day I kill every single pupil at St Sebastian's!'

William stopped halfway around the U-bend of the toilet.

Had he heard Edith right? She was going to kill the pupils of St Sebastian's? He knew she didn't like the noise of the children walking around the school above the sewer, but she'd never talked of murdering them before.

William had friends who went to the school. OK, they didn't know they were his friends because he had never appeared in front of them or tried to speak to them. But he liked to visit the school during the daytime and hang out with them all the same. He would miss so much about them if Edith managed to kill them all.

There was Alexander, the boy he looked eerily similar to. He was the cleverest person William had ever known and he told jokes, too. William often didn't understand them, but he knew they must be funny because other pupils laughed at Alexander wherever he went.

Lenny liked animals. William had been brought up on a farm and, although the only creatures he had contact with nowadays were sewer rats and leeches, he felt close to Lenny because of his love of nature.

James, the leader of the trio, was everything William wanted to be: handsome, witty, brave and – most of all – alive. He'd miss them all if Edith killed them.

Then there was Stacey to consider. No way could he allow Edith to bump off such a beautiful young girl.

Something had to be done. Something Edith wouldn't like one little bit.

Rising back up through the bubbling water of the toilet bowl, William was pleased to see that Stacey had finished changing her clothes and was now settled back on the bench, reading some sort of colourful parchment. It was now or never.

'Excuse me,' he said.

Stacey looked up.

William concentrated hard on appearing solid and tried to flatten down his untidy mop of hair.

'Alexander? Is that you?' asked Stacey.

'Er, no,' replied William. 'I do look a little like him, but my name is William. William Scroggins.'

Stacey threw down her magazine and jumped to her feet. 'What are you doing in the girls' changing rooms?' she demanded. 'I'll scream if you don't answer me!'

'It's OK!' insisted William. 'You don't have anything to fear from me – I'm dead!'

'D-dead?' stammered Stacey.

William grinned and nodded. 'For six hundred years,' he explained. 'The Black Death got me when I was about your age.' He knew that this would be an unusual thing for Stacey to hear, but he didn't expect the reaction he was about to get.

'Who put you up to this?' the blonde girl shouted. 'Do you go to St Mary's? Is that it? You just can't let go of the fact that our cheerleading team thrashed yours in the regional finals, can you? You'll be in trouble if one of our teachers finds you here. They're a lot stricter than the teachers at your pathetic school!'

'No, I really *am* dead!' said William, backing away from the furious girl. 'Look!'

To prove his point, William floated up into the air, became invisible once more and disappeared through the nearest wall.

When his head reappeared from the painted
brickwork, he found Stacey lying on the
changing-room floor, fainted out cold.

William drifted back into the room and landed silently beside her. 'This is going to be tougher than I thought!' he sighed.

CHAPTER 5
DOOMED!

'We're just twelve minutes into the first half and Gordon 'The Gorilla' Carver is making yet another break up the left wing!' Year-ten pupil Stuart Dixon continued his commentary of the year-seven versus year-eight football match over the newly repaired microphone.

'He's passed midfielder James Simpson, who tumbles into the mud as he stretches for the ball. Lenny Maxwell races up from defence, but Carver soon dispatches him with what appears to be an elbow in the face. Surely the referee will award a free kick? . . . No, he's waving "play on", and the only person who can now stop The Gorilla from making it three–nil is year-seven goalkeeper Alexander Tick.'

Alexander stared in horror as Gordon Carver angrily dribbled the ball towards him.

'Think happy thoughts,' said Alexander to himself. 'I know – Why was the football pitch shaped like a triangle? Because someone took a corner!' The joke did little to cheer the headmaster's son up in the face of The Gorilla's approach.

'Carver is ten metres from the year-seven goal. Eight metres. Will he shoot? No, he's just charged into Tick and knocked him to the ground before kicking the ball into his face. It's rebounded into the net – three–nil to year eight!'

James jogged over and helped the goalkeeper to his feet, as the year-eight team celebrated.

'Whose brilliant idea was it to put me in

goal?' asked Alexander. 'You might as well just ask me to stop a runaway train with my head!'

'It's not that we think you're any good in goal,' explained James, retrieving the ball from the back of the net. 'It's just that you're useless anywhere else. But you *nearly* stopped that one with your face.'

Alexander scowled. 'Thanks for the vote of confidence,' he groaned.

'Come on, Simpson!' roared Gordon Carver from the centre spot. 'Get the ball down here. I want to score again!'

'I'd better go and kick off,' said James to Alexander.

'Good idea,' came the reply. 'And why don't you swap the football for a bowling ball while you're at it? I think there's a couple of my bones The Gorilla hasn't broken yet!'

As James ran back to the centre circle, he passed Lenny. 'We have to try and keep the ball away from Gordon,' he said. 'I don't think Stick can take much more of this.'

'Neither can I,' added Lenny, rubbing at a bruise on his cheek where The Gorilla had elbowed him.

'And year seven kick off again,' echoed Stuart's voice over the sound system. 'Simpson to Maxwell, back to Simpson, who makes a break through the centre. He's brought down by Carver, who races back up the right wing, a clear run to the year-seven goal and a trembling Tick ahead of him.'

The crowd of parents on the touchline braced themselves for yet another scene of carnage, when Stacey pushed her way between them and on to the football pitch.

'Wait, there's someone on the pitch!' announced Stuart excitedly. 'It's Stacey Carmichael, and Gordon Carver has stopped in his tracks at the sight of her. Alexander Tick looks relieved – he thinks his pain is all over . . . It is now!'

'H–hello, Stacey,' mumbled Gordon, trapping the ball beneath his foot and smoothing down his football shirt. 'What a pleasant surprise!'

'We're all going to die!' screamed Stacey at the top of her lungs.

'What's going on?' demanded the science teacher, Mr Watts, who was refereeing the match. 'Miss Carmichael, you have no business on this football pitch. Please remove yourself immediately!'

'You don't understand,' wailed Stacey. 'I saw a ghost and he told me that we're all going to die!'

Lenny nudged James, who had climbed to his feet to watch Stacey's outburst. 'I think that bump on her head might have knocked her silly,' he said.

'Maybe,' answered James. 'It didn't look like Leandra hit her very hard, but then she is a delicate girl.'

44

The boys' conversation was interrupted by Mr Tick striding past them on to the pitch. He glared briefly at his son, now leaning against one of the goalposts and trying to catch his breath.

'I'll be discussing your goalkeeping skills with you later, young man!' he bellowed.

Alexander shuddered.

'Now then,' soothed the headmaster as he reached Stacey, 'what's all this about?'

'Oh, Mr Tick, sir!' she shouted. 'We have to abandon sports day!'

Mr Tick glanced nervously at the group of parents assembled to watch the game. 'Now, why would we want to do that?' he asked.

'Because a ghost told me that another ghost wants to kill us all!' Stacey sobbed, grabbing hold of the headmaster's jacket and twisting the material in her hands.

Mr Tick tried unsuccessfully to free himself from her grasp. 'Now then, er . . . Stacey, is it?

There's no such thing as ghosts!' he said, throwing the concerned parents a look which he hoped would say 'poor, confused girl'.

'He came out of the toilet!' replied Stacey, using the edge of Mr Tick's jacket to wipe her eyes.

The headmaster pulled it from her clutches in case she decided to blow her nose next. 'The toilet? I think we should get you back into the warm,' he said. 'Ms Legg will take you inside again.'

He was turning to walk away when Stacey flung herself to the ground and wrapped her hands around one of his legs.

'No!' she screamed. 'You have to listen to me! We're all doomed!'

'Get . . . off . . . me!' growled Mr Tick, as he tried to stride off, pulling the hysterical Stacey through the mud as he dragged his leg behind him.

The crowd of parents had now grown to include bemused pupils as well, and some were taking pictures on their camera phones.

'I don't want to die!' screamed Stacey, spitting
out a mouthful of mud. 'Please, Mr Tick – save
us from the ghosts!'

47

Mr Tick tried to free his leg from Stacey's grip, grinding the heel of his free foot into her fingers while smiling brightly at the parents. However, the girl's grip was too tight, and he was resigned to hobbling off the pitch with Stacey clinging to his leg, a forced smile fixed on his face.

Other sporting events were coming to a halt as word spread about the incredible scene being acted out on the football field. The 1,500-metre runners slowed to a stop to watch. A player in the year-nine tennis finals botched his serve. And a year-ten girl mistimed her javelin throw, spearing the podium from which the headmaster had made his speech and sending a flurry of teachers running for cover.

Mr Tick glowered down at Stacey, her face streaked with tears and mud. 'You'd better hope the ghosts do come and get you, young lady,' he snarled. 'Because if they don't, I will!'

CHAPTER 6
THE PLAN

Miss Keys burst through the double doors and out into the playground as fast as her sensible shoes would allow. The message had been clear: a pupil was attacking the headmaster. There was no way the school secretary was going to allow that to happen.

Mr Tick was, in her unbiased opinion, the greatest human being who had ever walked the earth. A giant among men – strict yet caring, disciplined yet understanding. And the way he could complete a game of solitaire with one hand while signing school budget cuts with the other . . .

Pounding across the grass now, the secretary spotted a crowd gathered on the football field. That had to be it. Ignoring the clumps of mud that were splashing up the back of her plain skirt and blouse, Miss Keys put her head down and ran.

'Let go!' shouted Ms Legg, as she gripped Stacey's ankles and tried to pull her away from the furious headmaster.

'No!' screamed Stacey, still clinging tightly to Mr Tick's left leg. Slowly but surely, the headmaster's trousers were starting to slide down. 'Not until he agrees to cancel sports day and sends us all home!'

Ms Legg shook her head and glanced up at Mr Tick with a nervous smile. 'I knew she wasn't

much of a fan of PE, sir, but she's never acted
like *this* before.'

'Get her off me, or I will have you on my list
for every miserable lunchtime and after-school
duty for the next five years!' growled the
headmaster, frantically clutching at his belt, not
wanting to reveal his favourite ace-of-spades
boxer shorts to the assembled crowd.

Ms Legg sighed, and pulled again.

Watching the human tug of war, James turned to Alexander. 'Does your dad always have to have women physically pulled away from him?'

'My Aunt Sheila had to drag my mum off him once, but that was because he'd taped the world solitaire finals over their wedding video, and she was trying to staple his ears to the wall.'

The boys watched in silence as Ms Legg continued trying to tear the sobbing Stacey away from the headmaster's trousers.

'This could *not* get any stranger,' said James.

'You'd think so, wouldn't you?' said Lenny, calmly, as he looked on.

Suddenly, with a wail like a scalded cat, Miss Keys dived through the crowd and landed on top of Stacey, successfully breaking the blonde schoolgirl's grip. The pair rolled about in the mud of the football pitch, screaming at each other.

'Right, that's *it!*' roared Mr Watts, throwing down his whistle. 'This match is abandoned!' He stormed off the pitch, mumbling something about 'crazy women' and 'I'll be in the pub' under his breath.

'Well, Stick, it looks like you're walking away from this game with all your internal organs intact,' said James, as Gordon Carver and his cronies stomped off to the dressing room, throwing Alexander a series of filthy looks.

The headmaster's son breathed a sigh of relief. 'If anyone finds a spine near the goalmouth, it's mine,' he said, rubbing at his bruised back.

Mr Tick reached down into the mud and pulled both Miss Keys and Stacey to their feet. 'Ms Legg,' he bellowed, 'take Stacey to my office and call her parents.'

The PE teacher grabbed the blonde girl's arm and began to march her away. The headmaster turned to his secretary.

'I suggest you go back to your office and think of a very good reason why I shouldn't call *your* parents!' he leant in and hissed at her.

Fighting back tears, Miss Keys nodded and hurried away. As she passed Stacey she jabbed the girl with her arm and sent her sprawling back into the mud with a squeal.

'This is turning into a sports day to remember,' said James.

'Indeed,' agreed Alexander. 'But it could be the last if Stacey is telling the truth.'

James stared at him. 'You think she really saw a ghost?'

Alexander shrugged. 'Can you think of another reason why she would allow herself to be dragged about in the mud?'

Leandra was helping Stacey back to her feet, her entire outfit covered in dirt.

'Please make them stop!' Stacey pleaded to her friend, mud clinging to her normally pristine blonde curls. 'They're going to kill us all!' Ms Legg gave Stacey's arm a tug and pulled her off in the direction of the changing rooms. Stacey's voice echoed as she was led away. 'Not there! Don't make me go back in there!'

Alexander turned to James and Lenny. 'Remember that time she dripped blue paint on her skirt in the art exam?' he asked. 'She nearly screamed the place down. Now she's coated in muck and for some reason she's not saying a word about it. Something's given her a fright, all right.'

'You think it could be the plague-pit ghosts from underneath the school?' asked James. Along with Lenny and Alexander, James had spoilt the ghosts' plans to close St Sebastian's several times.

'Perhaps,' said Alexander. 'But if it is them, they've turned it up a notch. They've never threatened to kill anyone before.'

'Maybe they're getting desperate,' suggested Lenny. 'When an animal becomes trapped, it will do almost anything in order to escape from predators. Sometimes even kill.'

'And the ghosts in the plague pit see us as predators?' asked James.

'We're a threat to their natural habitat,' answered Lenny.

'Their natural habitat is a smelly old sewer,' retorted James. 'You'd think they'd be glad to have a bunch of kids livening up the place above them.'

'They're supposed to be resting in peace after an agonising death at the hands of the Black Death,' said Alexander. He gestured to the heavy-footed pupils charging round the field in the sporting events that had now resumed. 'How peaceful can it be resting underneath *that* lot?'

'Then we have to be on our guard at all times,' said James. 'If there's one ghost up here, there could be more. And, by the sounds of things, they're not shy about making themselves known.' He turned to Lenny. 'What's next?'

His friend consulted the sports-day programme. 'Alexander's heading up the team for the swimming relay, I'm doing the one hundred-metres sprint, and you're in the discus tournament.'

'Right,' said James. 'Keep a sharp eye out for anything suspicious. If you see something, deal with it, then we'll report back here at the medal ceremony.'

James thrust a hand into the centre of their group, where it was joined by Alexander's and Lenny's. After a solemn moment of determination, the boys set off to compete in their events, knowing they may well have to defeat the ghosts as well as their sporting opponents.

CHAPTER 7
TO THE DEATH

William Scroggins eased his head out of the
toilet pipe and peered around the sewer. Empty.
He was safe. Squeezing the rest of his body out
of the constricting tube, he sighed with relief;
he had almost expected Edith to be waiting
for him.

He had taken three steps when he realised
that something was wrong. It was too quiet.
There were no animals in the tunnel. No rats,
leeches or cockroaches. Something was scaring
them away.

William started to run, when a hand shot out from the tunnel wall and grabbed his collar. He struggled to free himself of the vice-like grip, but he was held tight and could only watch in horror as Edith oozed out of the brickwork.

'So, how did it go?' she asked, smiling.

William swallowed hard. If things were bad when Edith shouted, they were much worse when she smiled.

'Fine,' he lied. 'They've started the sports day.'

'They *have*?' grinned Edith. 'How de*light*ful!' Her voice started to become more shrill. 'Perhaps you'd like to come and tell all your friends about your adventure?'

William smiled. 'I really don't think –'

'I said,' interrupted Edith, grabbing William's hair and pulling hard, 'perhaps you'd like to come and tell all your friends about your adventure!'

Without waiting for an answer, she dragged the boy along the tunnel and into the vast underground amphitheatre that the ghosts had built over the centuries under her guidance. It was filled to the brim with thousands of spirits, all of whom had died from the Black Death.

Sitting next to the upturned barrel that Edith used as a podium was the ghost of leech merchant Ambrose Harbottle. He looked up as William was hauled in his direction.

'Sorry,' he said, quietly. 'I did try and stop her, lad.'

Edith brought William to a halt in front of the assembled dead and pushed him forwards. 'Go on!' she screeched. 'Tell them what you told the blonde girl!'

William glanced nervously at the sea of faces in front of him. 'I, er . . .' he began.

'Speak up, Scroggins!' shouted Edith. 'We can't hear your treacherous words!'

William took a deep breath. 'I told her to warn the other children that Edith was planning to kill them!' he announced, then screwed his eyes shut and waited for the ghosts' attack.

It didn't come.

Slowly, William opened one eye. The spirits who filled the auditorium were muttering, and he could hear phrases like 'Fair enough!' and 'That's what I would have done!' echoing around the cavern.

Edith leapt out from behind the podium. 'What are you doing?' she screamed. 'You should be tearing the boy to pieces! He ruined our plans!'

A lone voice rang out from the horde of ghosts. '*Your* plans, Edith – not ours.'

'Who said that?' demanded the hag, ectoplasm flying from her mouth and covering the juicy leech which Ambrose was about to start sucking on. He tossed it away in disgust.

To the left of the auditorium, ghosts quickly began to edge away from the outspoken spirit, leaving one lone phantom, a xylophone made of ribs hanging limply around his shoulders. Edith advanced.

'Bertram Ruttle!' she hissed. 'What did you say?' The ghost sank back into his slime-coated seat as Edith towered over him.

'I, er . . . said that it was *your* plan to go up there and kill the children, Edith! Not ours. We shouldn't be taking the credit for such a wonderful idea!'

Satisfied, Edith turned away.

'But —' added Bertram.

Edith spun around, locks of her wiry, red hair waving around her face like fuzzy flames. 'But *what*?' she roared.

Bertram trembled, but figured that he was in trouble already. Actually voicing his concerns couldn't hurt now, could it? 'D–do we really have to kill them?' he asked. 'C–can't we just s–scare them away?'

Edith sucked in a deep breath and glared at him, but then realised that the ghosts around him were nodding their agreement. In a flash, she was back at her podium.

'So, you've all turned coward, have you?' she bellowed. 'You just want to frighten the little darlings in the hope that they'll leave and never come back?'

Murmurs of 'Yes!', 'That's it!' and 'Why not?' echoed around the amphitheatre. Edith's eyes began to glow red. Ambrose whimpered and stuffed a leech into each ear. The old hag was about to blow.

'*I'll* tell you why scaring the children won't work!' shouted Edith. 'I have been trying to frighten the children of St Sebastian's ever since it opened over a century ago, and it doesn't work! I have floated out of toilets, appeared in classrooms and materialised in corridors. I have possessed pupils and teachers alike, and I have changed into every terrifying form imaginable, from an alien to a zombie: even a school In-Spectre!'

Edith's audience was silent now, prisoners of her words. 'Children these days are impossible to scare! They watch horrifying stories on moving-picture boxes, and listen to music that battles its way up something called a chart!'

William stared at his fellow spirits in horror. They were taking all this in.

'These are not the children of our world, who spoke only with express permission from an adult,' continued Edith. 'These little monsters are encouraged to disagree with grown-ups and state their own points of view! They are taught to think for themselves!'

Her entire body now appeared to be pulsing with red light.

'*That* is why we cannot simply frighten the pupils of St Sebastian's. There's nothing we could ever do to scare them! No, they must be disposed of, and what an opportunity we have to do it! Not only do we get to dispatch every little brat who ever wore a school blazer but, assembled up there on the sports field right now, are their teachers and parents. The very people who *created* the little horrors!'

Everyone in the audience was captivated by her speech. Apart from William. He shook his head. He couldn't believe this was happening.

66

'So, get up there and attack, my ghostly friends! Attack every living thing until all is still and we can finally enjoy the peace and quiet we never received in life, but that we truly deserve in death!'

The amphitheatre shook as thousands of ghosts jumped to their feet and thundered their applause.

'No!' shouted William, trying to stop the crowds of spirits from racing out of the cavern and into the sewer tunnels. 'Stop! You can't do this!' But it was too late.

When Ambrose opened his eyes and pulled the leeches from his ears, he found he was alone in the amphitheatre. Unaware of the chaos that was beginning to unfold above him, he popped the leeches into his mouth and began to chew.

'Well,' he said to himself. 'At least everything's calmed down.'

CHAPTER 8
ATTACK!

James gripped the discus in his hand and scanned the crowd as he waited patiently for his turn to throw. Watching for creatures of the dead wasn't as easy as it sounded, especially when most of the parents looked as though they'd been dug up to come along and support the sports day.

'Next up in the discus,' announced the amplified voice of the commentator, Stuart Dixon, 'James Simpson from year seven.'

There was a smattering of polite applause as James stepped into the throwing circle and carefully positioned his legs. Time to forget about ghosts and just throw the discus. Once the event was over, he could concentrate on the matter at hand. Slowly, he began to spin.

It was as he completed his first turn that he saw the hand burst up through the soil at the end of the field. By the time he had spun around again, the entire upper half of the ghost was visible. After his third turn, the spirit had been joined by dozens of others.

Letting out a yell, James tried to stop himself from spinning around, but the momentum was too great. As he prepared to launch the missile, he spotted a grey-haired ghoul rushing towards him and, concentrating hard, James released the discus, hurling it in the direction of the approaching ghost

'Take that, you spook!' he shouted.

The heavy object flew through the air, almost in slow motion. It connected with the creature's

69

head, causing it to collapse to the ground, swearing loudly.

Swearing? James had expected the ghost to evaporate, or even to explode, not drop to the grass clutching at its head and cursing.

'Granddad!'

James froze. He knew that voice.

Gordon 'The Gorilla' Carver pushed past him and dropped to his knees beside the old man. Granddad? No, it couldn't be. Carver spun round and glared at him.

'You did that on purpose!' he roared. 'You deliberately threw the discus at my granddad!'

'Your granddad?' gulped James. 'I didn't realise! I–I thought he was dead!'

'I nearly was, thanks to you!' groaned the old man. 'I was only coming closer to take a picture!'

'It was an accident!' lied James. 'I thought I saw someone out there on the field, and I didn't want to hit them with the discus!' He pointed to the spot where the ghosts had been bursting up through the soil. There was nothing there.

'So you chucked it at my granddad instead?' yelled Carver. 'You'd better watch your back, Simpson, because Barry "The Butcher" Carver doesn't forget a face in a hurry!'

James swallowed hard as the bully helped his grandfather to his feet. 'The Butcher'? That didn't sound like the name of someone who would forgive and forget too easily. Both Carvers began to advance on him.

'I'm sorry, Mr Carver . . .' he began, backing away. 'I really thought you were something – I mean someone – else!'

Suddenly, a hand clamped down on his shoulder and he looked up. Mr Tick. James didn't think he'd ever be this relieved to see the headmaster.

'What's going on here?'

Spotting his chance to escape, James began to speak. 'It was my fault, sir! I wasn't concentrating and I threw the discus directly at Mr Carver. He probably wants to take legal action against the school, so I'd take me to your office for a stern punishment if I were you!'

Mr Tick blinked. A pupil *asking* to be disciplined? This was a new one. 'Well, maybe if you're prepared to apologise, I'm sure I could leave you here with Mr Carver to –'

'*No!*' interrupted James, as The Gorilla picked up the discus and began to slap it against his hand in a threatening fashion. 'I've been a very naughty boy and you should punish me. Come on!' James started to walk away, tugging at the headmaster's sleeve.

'I should, er . . . take him to my office,' he said, smiling politely at the Carvers as he was dragged away from the scene. This was turning into a very unusual day indeed.

Lenny grabbed his ankle and bent his leg backwards to stretch his muscles in preparation for the 100-metres sprint. Being tall and athletic, with long legs, he was incredibly fast. The hopes of a year-seven medal for this event were laid squarely at his size-ten feet.

'Hurry up, sir! I deserve a thousand lines at the very least!'

Lenny watched in amazement as James appeared to pull Mr Tick across the track towards the school. The headmaster stumbled after him, looking bemused.

Whatever James was up to, Lenny was sure he knew what he was doing, so he put the scene out of his mind in order to concentrate on the race ahead.

He slowly dropped to one knee and placed his foot against the starting block.

'You're a greyhound,' he said to himself. 'No, a cheetah – the fastest animal on the planet!'

'On your marks . . .' shouted Ms Legg, as the runners flexed their fingers against the cold grass.

Lenny glanced to his right, where Luke Thomas was poised, ready for action. If there was anyone he had to beat so as to win this race, it was Luke.

'Get set . . .' yelled Ms Legg.

Lenny pushed all thoughts of the day's events out of his mind and raised himself up into the starting position. He had a race to win, and he couldn't allow anything to distract him.

'*Go!*' screamed Ms Legg, over the sound of the starter's pistol.

Lenny launched himself forwards, stretching his legs out in the longest strides possible at the start of the race. It would all be over in a matter of seconds, and this was the best opportunity to secure a lead.

Legs pounding, Lenny focused on the red tape of the finish line fluttering in the wind, now just 80 metres ahead of him. He could hear feet thumping into the ground behind him and realised that he had taken an early lead.

Sixty metres to go. Voices cheered from alongside the track, but they seemed very far away. The loudest sound Lenny could hear was the rapid beating of his own heart.

Forty metres. Permitting himself a quick look around, Lenny saw that the only other runner with him was Luke Thomas. The boys were neck and neck as they closed in on the finish line.

Twenty metres. Lenny surged forwards and took a slight lead over Luke Thomas. This was it. The gold medal was his.

Just ten metres to go now.

Suddenly, a ghost shot up from the grass in front of him, playing some sort of musical instrument made of rib bones.

Lenny jumped and landed awkwardly on his right leg, twisting his ankle and crashing to the ground.

As Luke Thomas leapt over him and burst across the finish line, Lenny grabbed for his painful ankle and watched as the musical spirit sent the crowd running and screaming.

The attack had begun.

CHAPTER 9
WATER DISASTER

Alexander Tick stood at the edge of the swimming pool and stared into the water. He felt ridiculous, wearing only a tiny pair of trunks under his dressing gown. He had a horrible suspicion that he looked ridiculous, too.

'Would the contestants for the year-seven swimming relay please take their positions?' called out the maths teacher, Mr Parker. Alexander sighed heavily and, taking off his dressing gown, he stepped up to the starting block, ready for the race.

'Oi, Stick!' shouted a voice from the year-ten team. 'Shouldn't you be out on the field — as a javelin?' The crowd around the pool erupted into laughter, but Alexander tried to ignore them. All he had to do was two lengths of the pool, the next member of his team would dive in, and he could get dressed and get out of here.

The pool almost hadn't been ready for the sports-day events. Mr Wharpley had spent over an hour in his dad's office moaning about the broken filters and all the filth they'd thrown out into the water. But, after operating the pumps on full power for twenty-four hours — and using the school flag as a makeshift net — the caretaker had managed to get the pool clean just in time after all.

'He's so skinny that when he has a shower he has to walk around to get wet!' shouted another of the year-ten pupils. More raucous laughter echoed around the pool building.

Alexander positioned himself on the starting block and tried to ignore the taunts, while making a mental note to remember the jokes and add them to his humour database that evening.

'I bet if he goes outside when it's windy he twangs!' called a year-ten girl. More giggles filled Alexander's ears. All he had to do was look down and concentrate on the water. Once he was in there and swimming, he wouldn't be able to hear the teasing any longer.

The water. There was something wrong with the water. It was churning about. Barely visible figures were twisting in the water. *Ghosts!*

'On your marks!' called Mr Parker.

'No!' shouted Alexander.

'Get set!'

'Stop!' yelled Alexander.

'Go!'

Swimmers from years eight, nine and ten dived into the water. Alexander hesitated.

'Stop the race!' he called to the teacher, just as one of the girls from his year-seven team stepped forwards and pushed him into the pool.

'Get going, you idiot!' she shouted.

Alexander hit the water with a splash, and the chaos began.

Edith sat on the bottom of the pool and watched proudly as the spirits tugged at the pupils' legs, pulling them under and making them gasp for air each time they scrambled to the surface.

These ghosts were under strict instructions: they could terrorise the children all they wanted, but they had to stay invisible and couldn't begin the attack until Edith gave the order.

The swimmers couldn't see the ghosts, so they had no idea what was going on. To the onlookers it would seem as though the kids had dived in for the race, only to forget how to swim.

Edith laughed as a year-ten pupil kicked himself free of two elderly ghosts and tried to escape, but was caught by another, younger spirit. Soon, the boy was back under the water again, bubbles streaming from his mouth as he screamed for help.

Then, a real treat. Alexander Tick bellyflopped into the pool and began to splash around. That little know-all had ruined enough of Edith's plans for her to know who he was by sight.

'Leave that one to me!' she bellowed, shooting through the water like a torpedo.

Alexander saw the ripples caused by her movement and tried to kick back up to the surface. He was too slow and, within seconds, Edith was upon him.

'You're mine now, boy!' she mouthed, as she grabbed hold of Alexander's shoulders and pushed him down towards the bottom of the pool.

Alexander spun round in the water, his cheeks bulging as he fought to hold his breath. All he could see were slight disturbances in the water, and they were quickly masked by the splashes of the swimmers as they tried to escape.

Suddenly the tip of a lifesaving pole broke through the water's surface and appeared in front of Alexander's face. He reached out for it, not caring who was holding on to the other end, but grateful to them all the same.

Edith grabbed his hand and yanked it away, just as his fingertips touched the cold metal.

A year-nine girl managed to break free of Lady Grimes, her ghostly attacker, and gripped on to the pole. She was quickly pulled out of the water.

Alexander succeeded in scrambling to the surface for a brief second, just long enough to grab another mouthful of air and see that the caretaker, Mr Wharpley, was swinging the pole back over the water's surface.

Edith pulled him back down again, as the boy from the year-ten team was hooked by the loop at the end of the pole and pulled to safety. The ghost who had been holding him exploded in a rush of water as the boy's legs kicked right through him.

Edith laughed as Alexander's cheeks began to turn red, then purple. 'This is it, my pretty!' she whispered in his ear, materialising in front of him long enough for the boy to see the look of joy on her face. 'You're not going back to the surface!'

Alexander lashed out with his hands, trying to push the ghost away, but Edith's grip was strong, and the most he could do was wriggle around, which forced the last precious bubbles of air out of his lungs.

He watched as the year-ten swimmer was pulled from the pool, leaving him alone underwater with just Edith and her grisly ghosts. *I'm going to die*, he thought to himself. *I'm going to die before I get to take my GCSEs.*

As Alexander's vision began to blur, he found his strength sapping away, drop by drop. His chest was burning, and his brain begged him to take in a deep breath. Maybe that was the thing to do – just give in and breathe the water.

He was about to open his mouth when a blast of water jerked him back to reality. The pool was churning violently, and the ghosts were now fully visible, their concentration diverted from terrorising the pupils to their own safety instead.

They were being sucked backwards into the whirring filter fans and ripped into shreds of ectoplasm. Someone had turned the pumps on to full power!

Within seconds, the only ghost left in the water was Edith, her legs flailing about wildly as the fans in the pool filter pulled at her almost weightless body.

'Help meee!' she screamed to Alexander, but the boy just glared at her and used his last bit of energy to kick the ghost away. Edith spun backwards, squealing as she disappeared into the filter.

Alexander was sinking into blackness when several pairs of hands finally reached into the water and lifted him free of the pool.

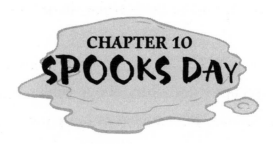

CHAPTER 10
SPOOKS DAY

'In all my years as a teacher, I have never witnessed a pupil attack a grandparent with a piece of sporting equipment!' said Mr Tick, as he sipped strong coffee from his prized 'Solitaire Champ' mug.

'You don't understand, sir,' explained James, standing on the other side of the headmaster's desk. 'When I attacked him, I didn't know he was a grandparent!' He thought for a moment before adding: 'That made more sense in my head than when I said it out loud, sir.'

'You clobbered Mr Carver with a discus, boy!' exclaimed the headmaster. 'This is a school — inflicting physical pain on others is just not sporting!'

Right on cue, there was a thump and a scream as Mr Hall, the history teacher, was slammed against the window of Mr Tick's office.

James stared as the teacher's agonised face slid out of view, leaving behind a trail of sticky saliva.

'You were saying, sir?' asked James.

'What in the name of the National Curriculum is going on out there?' roared the headmaster, jumping out of his chair and walking to the window.

James joined him. The entire sports field was overrun with ghostly figures causing mayhem.

The Headless Horseman had replaced his missing head with a rugby ball and was galloping across the cricket pitch. He was using a spine collected from the plague pit to play

polo with his own head, the one he normally kept tucked safely underneath his arm. Pupils dived out of the way as it screamed through the air at them.

Bertram Ruttle was in the midst of the 400-metres relay race, and had swapped each of the team's batons for a blood-soaked bone.

Aggie Malkin, a ghostly witch, had cast a spell over the sandpit at the end of the long jump, transforming it into a trap filled with quicksand.

She stood by and cackled as two year-nine girls were sucked slowly into it.

'They've started,' said James to himself.

The headmaster spun round to face him. 'Who's started?' he demanded. 'What do you know about this?'

'It's kind of difficult to explain, sir,' began James. 'You see, the school is built over a –' He stopped and stared beyond Mr Tick at something in the school playground. 'Oh, no!'

'What?' bellowed the headmaster. 'Why did you say "oh, no!"?'

'Things have just got worse, sir,' said James.

'How can they possibly get *worse?*' roared Mr Tick, but the sight of James's terrified expression caused him to turn and follow the boy's gaze out of the window.

A TV news crew was in the playground, busily unpacking their van.

'Oh, no!' echoed Mr Tick, quietly.

James crashed through the door and ran into the school playground just seconds behind Mr Tick. The headmaster raced for the TV news van, straightening his tie and trying to ignore the chaotic scene before him on the sports field.

The news reporter spotted Mr Tick and held out his hand. 'Richard Shaw, *Grimesford Today*,' he announced. 'But you can call me Rick!' The headmaster tried to catch his breath and introduce himself.

'Richard Tick,' he breathed heavily. 'Headmaster of St Sebastian's. *Never* call me Rick. I presume you're here to cover the school sports day?'

The reporter nodded. 'We don't normally attend stories as dull as this, but our director is a member of your Parent-Teacher Association, so we've no choice really.' He glanced around the playground, Mr Tick and James doing their best to keep themselves between the news team and the sports field. 'So, where would you like us to set up?' asked the reporter.

'Oh, there's no rush, is there?' oozed Mr Tick. 'Perhaps you'd like a tour of the school first? Or a cup of tea? Yes, that's it! Let's all go up to my office and have a nice cup of tea!' The headmaster glanced at the window of his office, remembering that it overlooked the sports field. 'No!' he blurted out. 'Not my office – the, er . . . science lab. Yes, that's on the other side of the school. Let's all go to the science lab for a cup of tea!'

'I think we should really get on and cover the events,' suggested Rick Shaw, smoothing his hair down with his hand as he checked his appearance in the van's wing mirror. 'What do you think, Steve?' There was no reply. 'Steve?' The reporter turned to his cameraman to find him staring open-mouthed across the sports field.

Children and parents alike were running in terror from a horde of ghosts who were chasing them with javelins.

'What the heck is going on there?' the cameraman asked.

Mr Tick laughed, nervously. 'Well, it's funny you should ask that,' he said. 'It's really quite a story . . . Yes, quite a story.' He whipped out a handkerchief to mop his sweating brow. 'And, er . . . James here will tell you that story! James?'

Everyone turned to face the eleven-year-old. He swallowed hard. 'Thank you, headmaster,' he began. 'I'd love to tell these gentlemen what's going on.' He paused briefly to allow Mr Drew, the music teacher, to run past, screaming. 'You see, they're, er . . . they're spooks!'

'Spooks?' asked Rick Shaw.

'Yes!' replied James, his eyes lighting up as an idea struck. 'Spooks! We decided that every other school has a plain, boring sports day, so we wanted to do something different. We got together, decided to give ours a ghostly theme, and called it the School Spooks Day!'

'Brilliant!' blurted out Mr Tick.

'Yes, it is,' said Rick Shaw, a smile spreading across his face. 'Here I was thinking I'd have to interview pupils about boring races and dull athletic events, but you've added a whole new

dimension by theming the entire affair!' He watched as a ghost wielding a dismembered arm chased a small crowd of parents past them. 'It all looks very realistic!'

'We've been working on the idea for some time,' said James, his voice filled with confidence now. 'Making props, designing costumes, that sort of thing. The entire school got involved, including the teachers and parents.'

'Well, what are we waiting for?' said Rick Shaw. He gestured to his cameraman, who hoisted a bag of equipment on to his shoulder, and the two men strode off in the direction of the sports field.

Mr Tick leant down to James and whispered in his ear. 'Whatever you get in this year's exams, it's just been doubled!'

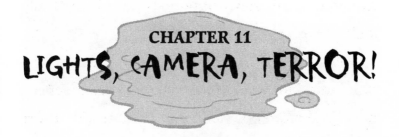

CHAPTER 11
LIGHTS, CAMERA, TERROR!

'And so, it is with great pleasure that we
welcome Mr Rick Shaw from our very own
local news programme, *Grimesford Today*!'
announced Mr Tick from his podium, sweat
pouring down his face. Around the field,
teachers, pupils and parents were battling with
ghosts from the plague pit. The headmaster
hoped they would buy into James's brainwave.

'We also hope you are enjoying our themed
sports day – School Spooks Day! A name, I'm
proud to say, that I came up with myself.'

James turned to Lenny, who was holding an ice pack to his swollen ankle. 'That name was *my* idea!' he said. 'Tick's just nicked it!'

The ghost of a burly farmer's wife lumbered past, heaving her husband's skull off her shoulder as though she was a shot-putter.

'I think we might have bigger problems,' suggested Lenny.

98

'So, join in with the fun, project a good image of St Sebastian's for the cameras and, most of all, enjoy our School Spooks Day!' finished the headmaster.

Around the field, the tense atmosphere dissolved. One by one, pupils, parents and teachers all came to the conclusion that somehow they alone had missed the letter explaining about this themed sports day.

A group of parents stopped running from the ghosts and began to compliment them on their costumes and make-up. Mrs Wordsworth, the English teacher, wrestled a bone out of Bertram Ruttle's hands and asked if he could provide props for the school's forthcoming production of *Hamlet*. And the two year-nine girls trapped in the long-jump sandpit stopped struggling and began to playfully throw quicksand at each other.

Sitting on top of a set of goalposts, invisible to everyone around him, William Scroggins watched as the plague-pit ghosts were transformed into a practical joke.

'Edith's not going to like this,' he said to himself.

Alexander slumped on to the damp grass next to Lenny and pulled his dressing gown even tighter around him. James examined his friend's expression.

'What happened to you?' he asked.

'Let's just say I'm not cut out to be a mermaid,' muttered the headmaster's son. He stared at the laughing parents and pupils as *they* now chased the ghosts around the field.

'Have I been transported to some sort of alternative universe – what's going on?' he asked.

'No,' said Lenny, carefully pulling a sports sock back over his injured ankle. 'James came up with the idea of telling everyone that the ghost attack is all make-believe.'

The boys watched as a group of year-ten boys raced after the Headless Horseman, the rugby ball still balanced on his shoulders.

'They think this is all staged?' said Alexander.

'Yep,' replied James, ducking as the horseman's real head was passed over them from one boy to another. 'And they've fallen for it, hook, line and sinker.'

Alexander leant back and rubbed a hand through his wet hair. 'Well, James,' he said, 'you've either saved us, or killed us.'

'What do you mean?' asked James.

'Think about it,' answered Alexander. 'That old crone who tortured me in the pool seems to be in charge. She won't be happy that her hordes of the dead have been made a laughing stock.' His expression darkened. 'Now she's got nothing to lose.'

'You idiot!' screamed Edith, her voice echoing around the empty amphitheatre beneath the school. 'My arms are the wrong way round!'

Ambrose Harbottle swallowed hard and stopped stitching Edith's leg back in place with a length of rotting string.

'I didn't say stop, *did I*?' yelled the hag.

Ambrose quickly pushed the makeshift bone needle through the ectoplasm of Edith's thigh and reattached the leg to her hip.

'I don't understand why you didn't just re-form on the other side of the fan in the pool filter,' said Ambrose, earning himself a slap across the side of his head.

'Because, you fool, I had Aggie Malkin cast a spell on the blades so that we could pass through them, but it seems it only worked going *in* to the pool. Whatever she did stopped me from sticking myself back together on the other side!'

Ambrose shuddered as he thought of the

punishment that awaited Aggie when she returned to the sewers. *I'm glad I'm not in her shoes*, he thought. Edith slapped him hard across the face again. It wasn't exactly fun being in his own shoes at the moment.

'My left leg is on backwards, you moron!' she yelled.

Ambrose threw down the needle and tried to stop his bottom lip from trembling. 'Look, I was a leech merchant, not a seamstress!' he shouted, folding his arms and sulking. 'If you want me to leave your other leg off until you find someone who can do a better job, just say the word!'

Edith sighed. The way Ambrose was putting her back together, she was starting to look like a circus freak but, until she could get Aggie to reverse whatever spell she'd cast on the pool filter, he was her only option.

'Oh, Ambrose,' she cooed, 'I'm not angry at you. I just want to be up there, taking part in the havoc we're wreaking on St Sebastian's.'

Ambrose turned, still sulking.

'Now, why don't you come back over here and help me reattach my other leg?' Edith continued. 'I'll make it worth your while. I'll tell you which leeches are Lady Grimes's favourites.'

104

The mention of Ambrose's love interest did the trick, and he bounded back over to Edith like an obedient puppy. 'I'll do a really good job on this leg!' he promised.

Edith smiled as the needle passed through her hip and the leech merchant got to work on her missing limb. 'That's more like it,' she said, patting him on the head.

Suddenly, Bertram Ruttle dashed into the cavern and began to root through a pile of half-buried skeletons. 'I need more bones!' he shouted over to Edith.

'I trust everything is going well?' she asked, grinning.

'Couldn't be better!' shouted Bertram, pulling an arm bone out of the soil. 'Haven't had this much fun in ages!'

'Good!' replied Edith. 'Tell me more . . .'

Bertram slung an almost complete skeleton over his shoulder and bounced over to Edith.

'I'm making props for the school play – and I might even get a part!' he announced, before racing out of the amphitheatre.

'*What?!*' screamed Edith, tightening her fingers in Ambrose's hair and wrenching out a fistful.

He winced as his body remembered the pain that he should have been feeling at that moment. He should have known Edith's kindness wouldn't last.

'Get my leg in place and get me up there!' she squealed.

Ambrose began to stitch faster. 'What are you going to do?' he asked, nervously.

'Whatever it takes,' Edith scowled.

CHAPTER 12
PLAYING DEAD

'You go first!'

'No, you go first!'

'You're the headmaster's son, I don't see why you shouldn't go first!'

'It's precisely *because* I'm the headmaster's son that I shouldn't go bursting in there!'

'Will you two stop bickering?' hissed James to Lenny and Alexander. '*I'll* go first!' He pushed the door to the girls' changing rooms open a fraction and pressed his mouth to the gap. 'Leandra!' he called. 'Are you in there?'

107

The door to the changing rooms was yanked inwards and all three boys tumbled forwards. Leandra glared at them.

'If you're trying to get a peek, there's a broken window round the other side!' she snapped.

'It's nothing like that!' said Lenny. 'We need your help.'

'I can't do anything at the moment,' replied his sister. 'I'm keeping watch for Stacey while she's in the shower.'

'How is she?' asked James.

'Moaning about how it'll take a year of washing to get the mud out of her hair,' said Leandra.

'Well, at least she's back to normal,' said Alexander.

'It's the ghosts, Leandra,' explained James. 'The ghosts from the plague pit. They're attacking the sports day and we think it might get worse at any moment.'

'They've threatened to kill us all,' said Lenny.

Leandra paled slightly. Being stuck in the girls' changing rooms with Stacey, she'd been unaware of all the mayhem going on outside. 'What can we do?'

James shrugged. 'Not a great deal — there are too many of them for us to deal with on our own. I guess, we just keep an eye on everyone and make sure they're OK.'

Leandra gestured inside the changing rooms. 'What about Stacey?'

'She's washing her hair,' said Alexander. 'She'll be at least four hours!'

Leandra nodded and stepped out of the changing rooms to follow James, Lenny and Alexander out on to the sports field. Had she turned back, she might have noticed a thin, red-headed figure with one leg pointing in the wrong direction and odd arms standing just behind her.

'And how long did you spend on your costume for the event?' asked Rick Shaw.

Lady Grimes blushed. 'Oh, I didn't make this myself,' she said into the opening of the magical picture-grabber. 'My ladies in waiting had this delivered from Dunbobbin's of London in thirteen forty-nine!'

Rick Shaw whispered to Steve, the cameraman, 'Keep rolling. She's good!'

'And what was it that made you want to take part in today's events?' he continued in his best on-air voice.

'Edith,' explained Lady Grimes. 'She threatened to make every day of my death absolute hell if I didn't get up here and attack the living.'

'And cut!' said Rick Shaw. Steve stopped filming and lowered the camera. 'That was great,' said the reporter, pulling out a notepad.

'Now, can I take your real name for the on-screen graphics?'

The ghost sniffed. 'Lady Petronella Grimes!' she announced, before striding away, nose in the air.

'Whichever amateur dramatic company this lot are from, they deserve some sort of award,' said Rick Shaw.

'You think she was good, look at this one!' said Steve, switching his camera back on and pointing it at the deformed figure of Edith as she came hobbling across the field, her face a picture of pure fury.

'Excuse me, miss, can we have a few words?' enquired the reporter.

Edith threw him a look as she limped by. 'Go and eat goat dung!' she roared.

'Well,' said Steve, lowering the camera and turning to face the surprised reporter, 'you did ask for a few words.'

'Are you OK?' asked James, as he and Leandra struggled to pull one of the two year-nine girls out of the quicksand in the long-jump pit.

'I was for the first few minutes after we found out it was all planned,' replied the girl. 'But I still can't move my legs and I'm starting to get cramp. What *is* this stuff?'

'Er, something they cooked up in the kitchen,' lied Leandra. 'They mixed porridge in with the sand.'

With a sound like a vomiting vacuum cleaner, she and James managed to pull the girl to freedom.

'Me next!' shouted the other girl. 'I can't feel my feet any more!'

James and Leandra moved over to her and started to pull.

Behind them, unnoticed, William Scroggins materialised. He glanced back across the sports field to where Edith was shambling from ghost to ghost, ordering the slaughter of all the St Sebastian's pupils. He had to act now, or it would be too late.

Ambrose had often pointed out to him that he looked a lot like Alexander, the headmaster's son. Here was his chance to put this to the test.

'I've got an idea,' he said, crouching down behind James and Leandra as they tugged at the year-nine pupil. James glanced briefly over his shoulder at William.

'Stick, you're supposed to be over on the archery range with Lenny!' he groaned.

William smiled to himself. It was working! 'I know,' he continued. 'But I think I know how we can make the ghosts go away.'

'Tell us then,' said Leandra, ignoring the tearing sound that was coming from the year-nine girl's T-shirt as she pulled.

'If the ghosts want us to die, we'll do just that,' explained William, trying his hardest to sound like Alexander. 'If we all play dead, they might just think they've succeeded in killing us and head back down to the plague pit.'

114

James paused to catch his breath and think for a second. 'That's brilliant!' he said, turning to congratulate Alexander. But there was no one there.

'What's happening now?' asked Rick Shaw, as his cameraman slowly panned across the sports field. One by one, the pupils, teachers and parents were screaming in agony and dropping

to the ground. Luckily, the camera's microphone wasn't quite sensitive enough to capture the whispers of 'Play dead, pass it on!' that were causing the spectacle.

Within minutes, everyone at the sports day had pretended to die an agonising death – some making more of a meal of it than others – and the entire field was littered with bodies. The plague-pit ghosts stopped in their tracks and stared.

'We've done it!' roared Edith. 'We've won!'

A grisly cheer went up around the field as the ghosts realised that Edith's obsession with the school would finally be at an end.

'To the pit, where we shall celebrate with dancing and leech wine!' cried Bertram Ruttle.

Another cheer echoed around the sports field and, one by one, the ghosts began to turn invisible and sink back into the ground.

'This is *great*!' Rick Shaw exclaimed to Steve. 'Are you getting all this?'

But the cameraman was on his knees, fumbling about in his bag.

'No – the blooming battery's died,' he said, apologetically.

Rick Shaw looked around for some movement. 'I wonder if we can get them to do it again on film?' he thought aloud.

Mr Tick was the first to spring back to life and climb to his feet. 'Bravo!' he shouted, rousing the other corpses from their imaginary slumber. 'What a performance!'

Slowly, the applause spread across the field. James and Leandra joined Lenny and Alexander.

'Of all the ideas you've ever had, that one has to be the best!' announced James to the headmaster's son.

Alexander stopped clapping and looked blank. 'What idea?' he asked.

CHAPTER 13
GRIMESFORD TODAY

James and Lenny joined Alexander on the raked seating in the school hall for the special assembly called by Mr Tick.

The headmaster paced, expressionless, as the pupils filed in.

'What's he going to say?' James asked Alexander.

'He wouldn't tell me,' came the reply. 'But by teatime last night he'd convinced himself that it was all a practical joke organised by pupils who wanted to make St Sebastian's look ridiculous for the cameras.'

'He seemed quite happy with it when he was applauding and shouting "Bravo!" yesterday,' said James.

'I think that's just because that reporter was still there,' said Alexander. 'He didn't want to look as though it had all been arranged behind his back.'

'Well, whatever he's going to say, he'd better hurry up,' moaned Lenny. 'This is cutting in to my lunchtime!'

James and Alexander did their best to hide their smiles.

'Right, settle down everyone,' ordered Mr Tick, after the last of the pupils had taken their seats. 'As I'm sure you're aware, the school was terrorised yesterday – not by ghosts, but by certain pupils who were determined to tarnish the good name of St Sebastian's by staging this elaborate hoax.'

The assembled pupils glanced at each other, surprised to hear that the spooky theme hadn't been planned in advance after all.

'I'm not an unreasonable man,' continued Mr Tick – the pupils and teachers silently disagreeing with him – 'but I will not stand for such unruly behaviour! If the culprits are willing to come forwards, I shall see to it that their punishment is not as severe as it would otherwise be.'

Again, everyone in the hall looked around, waiting to see if anyone would own up to hiring several dozen actors and providing them with ghost costumes and make-up just to get out of running a 400-metre race.

'You know,' whispered Alexander to James, 'if we were to own up to arranging this, we'd get into trouble – but we'd also go down in history for staging the most elaborate school joke of all time!'

'Keep your hand *down*!' hissed James.

At the front of the hall, Mr Tick sighed. 'Very well,' he said. 'I see that I shall have to employ a little detective work to uncover the ruffians behind this nonsense. And there will be no outdoor break time until the matter is resolved. You are all confined to your classrooms, where you will undertake extra written work.'

The hall was filled with moans and comments of 'Sir!', 'That's not fair!' and 'You can't do that!'

Mr Tick raised his hands to silence the pupils. 'Now, if you will all make your way back to your classrooms,' he said, just as a flushed-looking Miss Keys came rushing into the hall.

'It's on!' she squealed, excitedly.

'What's on?' asked Mr Tick.

'The school!' answered the secretary, jumping up and down, eagerly. 'We're on the lunchtime edition of *Grimesford Today*!' She raced over to the corner of the room and switched on the

TV normally reserved for documentaries about the Welsh fishing industry and infectious diseases. Rick Shaw appeared on the screen.

'We're here at St Sebastian's School in Grimesford, where the annual sports day has been hijacked!' he announced, as the camera panned around to reveal the plague-pit ghosts terrorising the pupils and staff.

Mr Tick sighed and looked away.

'Hijacked by a level of excitement this reporter has not seen at a school event in a long time,' continued Rick Shaw. 'Whoever decided to theme what could have been a run-of-the-mill sports day and turn it into a ghostly costumed event deserves congratulations. The entire school threw themselves enthusiastically into the proceedings, resulting in a triumph for athletic achievement and freedom of expression.'

As the report continued, the TV showed various scenes from the sports day, closing with

the sight of the pupils, teachers and parents
dropping down 'dead'.

'So, well done to the staff of the school for
allowing their pupils to really go to town. This is
Rick Shaw at St Sebastian's School for *Grimesford
Today*. Back to you in the studio, Mike . . .'

Miss Keys switched off the television and the
entire school held its breath while it waited for
the headmaster's reaction.

'Well,' he began, 'as you can see, you're not the only ones able to pull off a prank. I hope you all enjoyed my little joke earlier about punishing whoever was responsible for all of this.'

The pupils breathed a sigh of relief.

'And I'm delighted that whoever overheard my idea to turn the sports day into a school spooks day took it upon themselves to run with it,' he continued. 'Yes, my idea . . .'

'Does this mean that we're allowed outside at break again, Mr Tick?' called a voice from the year-ten row.

'Of course!' beamed the headmaster. 'As soon as the bell goes, you're all welcome to head out for a breath of fresh air!'

James swung his bag over his shoulder and turned to Lenny and Alexander.

'You coming?' he asked. Lenny nodded, but Alexander shuddered and sank further down into his chair.

124

'Not me,' he said. 'I've had enough fresh air to last me a lifetime!'

In the sewer deep below the school, Edith Codd settled back into the deckchair that Bertram Ruttle had built for her out of discarded bones and sighed, contentedly.

'Ahhh, this is the death!' she said, reaching out for her cup of leech wine, her limbs now the right way round thanks to a little magic from the sewer's resident witch, Aggie Malkin. All she had to do was relax and let the spell do its work, and relaxing was something she would be doing a lot more of from now on. She had peace, quiet and a total lack of children to spoil her mood.

Suddenly, a muffled bell rang out above her and hundreds of pairs of feet jumped to the floor, clattering about noisily. Pieces of mud and stone fell down from the amphitheatre ceiling on to Edith. She jumped to her feet.

'*What?*' she screamed. 'They were all dead! I saw them! How the plague can they be back at school today?'

A large brick worked loose from the mortar and fell from above, slicing through her ectoplasmic body and severing an arm that hadn't quite set in place yet. It landed in a puddle of mud with a splash.

Edith Codd glared up towards the school and shrieked so loudly that her voice rattled through every tunnel and pipe in the sewer. 'I haven't finished with you yet, St Sebastian's! I haven't finished with you at all!'

SURNAME: Maxwell

FIRST NAME: Leonardo (otherwise known as Lenny)

AGE: 11

HEIGHT: 1.7 metres

EYES: Brown

HAIR: Brown and curly

LIKES: Animals. Lenny has his own animal hospital in his bedroom, where he nurses sick and injured birds, mice, squirrels and rats back to health before setting them free in his back garden. Also has a pet rat, Whiskers

DISLIKES: His big sister Leandra making him look silly in front of Stacey

SPECIAL SKILL: Looking tougher than he really is. Using his pets to help save the day

INTERESTING FACT: Lenny holds the unofficial record at St Sebastian's for eating the most helpings of school dinner at one sitting

For more facts on Lenny Maxwell, go to **www.too-ghoul.com**

Alexander Tick's
Joke File

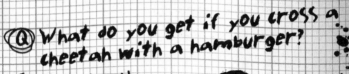

Q What do you get if you cross a cheetah with a hamburger?

A Fast food!

Q Where do pirates go shopping?

A Arrrr-gos!

Q Why doesn't Dracula have any friends?

A Cos he's a pain in the neck!

Q What do you call a prehistoric ghost?

A A terror-dactyl!

NOTE TO SELF: input these into jokes database at earliest convenience

Knock Knock

Who's there?

Armageddon...

Armageddon who?

Armageddon outta here!

Q What cheese is made backwards?
A Edam!

Q What did the ghost read every day?
A The horror-scope!

Q What did the guitar say to the rock star?
A Stop picking on me!

Q What's grey and squirts jam at you?
A A mouse eating a doughnut!

To see some of Alexander's joke database, visit: www.too-ghoul.com

Leeches of the British Isles

By Ambrose Harbottle

Leechius maximus

A big, juicy leech, perfect for sucking the blood out of children's legs. Found in murky swamps.

Leechius crunchius

A hard-boned leech that makes the perfect mid-morning snack. Best eaten raw, in one go. *

Leechius minimus

This leech is perfect for packing in a first aid kit, in case an emergency bleeding is needed on a country walk.

Leechius sillius

This leech gets its name from the ridiculous shape of its head. It is often found hidden under leaves in dark swamps.

Leechius slimius

A slippery leech found slithering over tree roots in marshy lowlands. Tastes great in cheese sandwiches.

Leechius chewius

A tasty, chewy leech that lasts for ages and ages. Can be taken out of the mouth and stuck behind the ear to be saved for later. Or flicked at girls when they aren't looking.

Always consult an adult before going leeching. Some leeches can be poisonous.

*May contain nuts

SPORTS DAY DEFENCE

How to defend your school sports day from ghostly attack, by James, Lenny and Alexander

Part 1: WEAPONS

1. **THE JAVELIN**
   Perfect in case of a vampire invasion during sports day. Use as a spear to throw through their hearts. Note: don't practice this on your classmates beforehand.

2. **THE DISCUS**
   This can be used to slice the heads off a marching zombie army as they advance across the playing field. Should not be thrown at bullies' grandads' heads.

3. **SHOT-PUT**
   Use this to knock out a headless horseman. It should keep him still long enough for you to nick his head and run away.

4. **STARTING PISTOL**
   Ghostly armies usually use swords and shields and are scared of new weapons, like guns. Fire it off a few times, then leg it like you really have just started a race!

5. **RUNNING TRACK**
   Less of a weapon, more of an escape route. If all else fails, hotfoot it well away from any medieval plague pits or burial grounds!

Medieval Sports FACTS

Forget the egg-and-spoon race. Which sports would the ghosts have been playing when they were alive?

You couldn't buy footballs in medieval times. People used inflated pigs' bladders instead!

Jousting was a popular sport. Two knights would ride towards each other on horses and try and knock each other off with long poles.

Everyone had to practice archery by law in medieval times. And no, you weren't allowed to use your headmaster as a target . . .

There were no computer games in the fourteenth century. If you were lucky, you might have some dice and a spinning top to play with!

Football was popular, but not as we know it. Whole villages would play against each other with teams of fifty people – and no rules or referees!

In 1409, king henry IV tried to ban football in England. Luckily, he didn't succeed.

Tennis was invented in medieval times. Originally, people would use their hand to hit the ball. Racquets weren't invented until later on.

Other popular sports included fighting animals – like bears. These cruel sports were banned long ago though.

Can't wait for the next book in the series?

Here's a sneak preview of

GHOUL DINNERS

available now from all good bookshops,
or **www.too-ghoul.com**

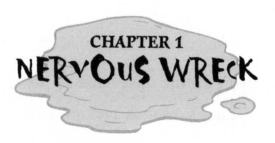

CHAPTER 1
NERVOUS WRECK

Mrs Cooper, St Sebastian's longest-serving dinner lady, was singing happily to a song on the radio. A huge vat of bolognese sauce bubbled on the cooker top, and the kitchen was filled with the rich smell of tomatoes. She danced across to the huge fridge, her bottom swaying as she moved in time to the music, shaking a jar of oil in one hand like a maraca.

'Cheese . . . that's what I need . . .' Mrs Cooper sang, as she grabbed the door handle. The door swung open and icy vapour curled out of the fridge. 'Funny . . . I must have the setting too cold . . .' she muttered to herself, pulling the door open wide.

She shrieked as she came face to face with a severed head, sitting on the top shelf. It dripped blood on to the shelves below. The head blew her a kiss, and winked.

'Hello, darling!' a raspy male voice laughed.

Mrs Cooper dropped the jar of oil and it shattered on the floor with a crash. Mrs Meadows, her fellow dinner lady, rushed into the kitchen carrying a huge bag of frozen chips.

'What's the matter, love? Did you cut yourself?' She rushed over to Mrs Cooper's side. 'I heard you scream . . .'

'It's . . . it's . . .' Mrs Cooper pointed at the fridge with a shaking finger. Mrs Meadows nudged her out of the way.

'Can't see anything that bad, Lynn. There's a mouldy-looking piece of cheddar but we can cut the edges off . . .' she rummaged further.

'But there's a – a head!'

'Of slimy lettuce. Yes, I know – if the headmaster sees it we'll get another lecture about "the importance of running a tight ship", but it's not *that* bad. Here! I'll stash it in the bins.'

She bustled past Mrs Cooper who was still staring at the fridge, wide-eyed. 'You have a sit-

down, love,' Mrs Meadows frowned. 'I'll pop
the kettle on for a brew – that'll make you
feel better!'

Mrs Cooper sat down heavily. Her eyes kept
darting back to the fridge. The kettle started to
boil with a loud whistle and she jumped out of
her seat.

'You are jittery this morning, Lynn! What's
wrong?' Mrs Meadows asked, turning off the
kettle and putting her arm around her friend.

'N–n–nothing, Sue!' Mrs Cooper smiled,
bravely. 'Just my imagination playing tricks
again.' She shook her head and her perm bobbed
up and down. 'Our Alex had us all awake late
last night playing his flaming rock music. I'm just
tired, that's all!' she laughed shakily and got up.

'Oh – don't get me started on teenagers! Our
Joanne has me in a flap most days. Kids! Come
on – I'll make that tea. Then we'd better get the
fryer going for these chips.'

Mrs Cooper looked over her shoulder towards the fridge and shuddered, then she turned on the tap to fill a huge pan with water for the spaghetti.

Deep in the store cupboard, something was stirring. A mouse nibbled at the corner of a packet of raisins and squeaked with excitement as the brown treasures tumbled out of the hole. It didn't notice the green, glowing mist that slid along the shelf behind it. The mouse stuffed its cheeks happily with sweet treats.

The mist rose until it towered over the creature. It started to take on a shape: first a fat, furry body and then a long, fluffy tail, next came four paws with long, razor-sharp claws and, finally, a face topped by pointed ears and a mouthful of teeth like daggers.

The mouse stopped eating. Its whiskers twitched and it cocked its head on one side to listen. A strange, rumbling sound filled the store cupboard. It had heard that noise before – it was the sound of a cat purring!

The mouse spun round to see green eyes glittering in the darkness. A huge paw shot out and stamped on its tail. The mouse was trapped. It pulled and squeaked, its heart beating fast. It gave an almighty heave, and its tail stretched thin.

At that moment, the cat lifted a paw and the mouse shot away across the cupboard, hitting packets as it fell, like a furry ball in a pinball machine. The cat seemed to smile, and then started to dissolve back into mist. It liked torturing small, defenceless things. And dinner ladies.

Back in the kitchen, Mrs Cooper was whisking a bowl of chocolate mousse. After her cup of tea, she felt much better. She poured the sticky mixture into lines of plastic pots. Putting the bowl in the dishwasher, she opened the store-cupboard door.

'Hmmm, where did I put those pots of sprinkles . . .? Oh — these will do!' she grabbed a large plastic tub of jelly drops. 'I hope there's enough left . . .' she raised the tub to look and screamed. It was a jar of eyeballs!

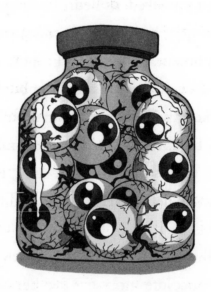

Mrs Cooper dropped the tub and ran backwards and forwards in the cupboard in blind panic. She knocked bottles and jars off shelves and as she fell back on to a tall, wobbly set of shelves, a bag of flour toppled over and covered her in a white cloud.

Mrs Meadows came barrelling in to the cupboard and grabbed Mrs Cooper, who screamed even louder.

'Lynn! It's me! Calm down!'

'Eyes! Eyeballs! They were looking right at me . . .' Mrs Cooper groaned and swayed. Mrs Meadows steered her back into the kitchen.

'Sit there!' she ordered, picking up the phone and ringing Mr Wharpley, the school caretaker.

'Reg? It's Sue here, in the kitchen. I need your help. No, nothing's broken – well, nothing I can't deal with,' she sighed, looking at the broken jars and bottles on the floor of the store cupboard. 'It's Lynn. She's ill, and I need someone to drive her home. Thanks, Reg. Yes, I owe you a chocolate fudge cake for this!' she smiled.

She put the phone down and bobbed down next to her friend. 'I think you need a rest, love.

Reg is going to take you home, and I'll ring your Kev at work to let him know you're poorly.'

Mrs Cooper stared past Mrs Meadows, chewing her lip. 'Eyeballs . . .' she whispered.

Moments later, Mr Wharpley and Mrs Meadows steered the shaking dinner lady into Mr Wharpley's van.

As it pulled away from the kerb noisily, Mrs Meadows sighed. 'Poor Lynn!' She shook her head. 'And poor me!' she groaned.

Then she trudged back to the kitchen to prepare three hundred portions of chips by herself.

The next day, the headmaster, Mr Tick, was humming to himself as he played solitaire on the computer in his office. A cup of coffee steamed on his desk, and Miss Keys had left a plate of his favourite crumble creams within easy reach. All was well with the world.

Mr Tick looked up, thinking hard about his next move, when he saw a shadow through the frosted glass in his office door. He sighed and his shoulders sagged. He opened the Department for Education web page to hide his game of solitaire and called, 'Enter!'

His secretary, Miss Keys, scuttled in, biting her lip nervously.

'Well? What is it? Something important to justify disturbing my work, I presume . . .?' Mr Tick growled.

'Erm, I'm afraid Lynn Cooper has just rung to say she won't be in today and won't be back in the foreseeable future. Well, it was her husband, actually. He said she was very poorly and couldn't come to the phone. The doctor has signed her off work with her nerves.'

'Well, he couldn't sign her off without her nerves, could he?' chuckled Mr Tick at his own joke.

143

Miss Keys looked puzzled.

Mr Tick sighed. 'I don't know why I bother . . .' he grumbled under his breath and frowned. 'Lynn Cooper? I don't remember any teachers called Lynn Cooper . . .'

'Erm, she's not a teacher, Mr Tick. She's a dinner lady. She works in the kitchen.'

'Ah – of course!' Mr Tick nodded, his eyes blank. 'Her nerves, you say? How frightening can a vegetable rack get? How scary can a deep fryer be?' he chuckled at his own jokes.

Miss Keys just looked at him, baffled.

'I'm wasted here,' he sighed to himself. 'So, off on account of her nerves for the foreseeable future, eh? Hmm . . . We'll have to advertise straight away for a replacement.' He sighed deeply.

Mr Tick pulled his gold–plated fountain pen out of his top pocket and scribbled details of the advertisement on a piece of school notepaper.

The pen left huge blobs on the paper that dribbled as he handed the sheet to Miss Keys.

'There you go! Type this up ASAP, Miss Keys! We can't have the school kitchen grinding to a halt, can we? We'll end up with one of those fussy celebrity chefs swooping down on the school and banging on about healthy eating if we're not careful!' he chuckled.

Miss Keys looked even more confused.

Mr Tick rubbed his forehead wearily. 'The advertisement, please?' he sighed.

Miss Keys scampered off to her desk and began to type. She read the words carefully and checked them twice. She pressed 'print'. At that moment, Mr Tick took a huge slurp of his coffee and realised it had gone cold. Gagging, he shouted for Miss Keys. 'This coffee is cold! Really, Miss Keys! This will not do!'

The secretary scurried off to the coffee machine and rushed back in to the headmaster's

145

office with a steaming fresh cup. A gust of wind pushed its way in through the open window. It tickled the papers on Miss Keys's desk, lingering over the advertisement.

Then, caught by the wind, the advertisement flew into the air and danced out of the window, eventually coming to rest on the sports field.

Miss Keys stumbled back to her desk, pink-cheeked and embarrassed. Fancy letting Mr Tick's coffee get cold! *I hope Lynn's nerves aren't catching!* she shuddered.

She reached for the advertisement. It wasn't there.

I could have sworn *I'd printed that already* ... Miss Keys shivered, closing the window against the chill.